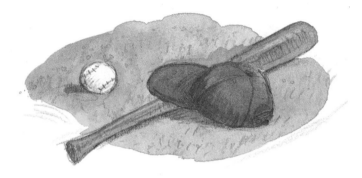

A NOTE TO PARENTS

When your children are ready to "step into reading," giving them the right books is as crucial as giving them the right food to eat. **Step into Reading Books** present exciting stories and information reinforced with lively, colorful illustrations that make learning to read fun, satisfying, and worthwhile. They are priced so that acquiring an entire library of them is affordable. And they are beginning readers with a difference—they're written on five levels.

Early Step into Reading Books are designed for brand-new readers, with large type and only one or two lines of very simple text per page. **Step 1 Books** feature the same easy-to-read type as the Early Step into Reading Books, but with more words per page. **Step 2 Books** are both longer and slightly more difficult, while **Step 3 Books** introduce readers to paragraphs and fully developed plot lines. **Step 4 Books** offer exciting nonfiction for the increasingly independent reader.

The grade levels assigned to the five steps—preschool through kindergarten for the Early Books, preschool through grade 1 for Step 1, grades 1 through 3 for Step 2, grades 2 through 3 for Step 3, and grades 2 through 4 for Step 4—are intended only as guides. Some children move through all five steps very rapidly; others climb the steps over a period of several years. Either way, these books will help your child "step into reading" in style!

Text copyright © 1998 by Sharon Dennis Wyeth.
Illustrations copyright © 1998 by Lynne Woodcock Cravath.
All rights reserved under International and Pan-American Copyright Conventions.
Published in the United States by Random House, Inc., New York, and simultaneously
in Canada by Random House of Canada Limited, Toronto.

http://www.randomhouse.com/

Library of Congress Cataloging-in-Publication Data:
Wyeth, Sharon Dennis.
Tomboy trouble / by Sharon Dennis Wyeth ; illustrated by Lynne Woodcock Cravath.
    p. cm. — (Step into reading. A step 3 book)
SUMMARY: When Georgia, an eight-year-old girl, cuts her hair very short and plays baseball,
the children in her new school ask her if she's a boy.
ISBN 0-679-88127-1 (trade) — ISBN 0-679-98127-6 (lib. bdg.)
[1. Sex role—Fiction. 2. Self-acceptance—Fiction. 3. Schools—Fiction. 4. Moving,
Household—Fiction.]
I. Cravath, Lynne Woodcock, ill. II. Title. III. Series: Step into reading. Step 3 book.
PZ7.W9746Gk 1998 [E]—dc20 96-41723

Printed in the United States of America 10 9 8 7 6 5 4 3 2 1

Step into Reading®

TOMBOY TROUBLE

By Sharon Dennis Wyeth

Illustrated by Lynne Woodcock Cravath

A Step 3 Book

Random House 🏠 New York

1
Georgia

My name is Georgia. I am eight. I am a girl. This is my story.

It was summer. I had long hair. When I played baseball, I got hot. Very hot. I was sweating!

So I got a haircut.

The hair cutter was a man. I liked his tie.

"How short do you want it?" the hair cutter asked.

"Short," I said.

"How short?" asked Mommy. She was there, too.

"Pretty short," I said.

"This short?" asked the hair cutter.

"Shorter," I said.

"Maybe not *that* short," said Mommy.

"I want to see my ears," I said.

"Your ears?" said Mommy. "Really?"

"Yes."

The hair cutter cut. He cut a lot. I could see my ears. They looked nice.

"All done," said the hair cutter.

"Wow!" I said.

"That's *short,* Georgia," said Mommy.

"I like it," I said.

Mommy paid the hair cutter. Someone swept up my old hair. Mommy looked sad.

"Don't worry," the hair cutter told Mommy. "It will grow back."

"I don't want it to grow back," I said.

We went outside. The weather was warm, but I felt cool.

"When I was a little girl," said Mommy, "I wanted long hair."

I put on my baseball cap. "Not me."

"I didn't want my ears to show," said Mommy.

"Why not?" I asked.

Mommy said she didn't like her ears.

"Poor Mommy," I said.

I passed a store. I saw myself in the
window. I took off my hat.

I looked great! It was the best haircut I
had ever had.

2
The Line

Summer was over. My family had moved.

I went to school. A new school. At my new school, there were two lines. A line for the girls and a line for the boys.

I had to stand in the girls' line. Because I'm a girl.

At my old school there was one line for everybody.

A boy had a baseball cap on, just like mine. He waved at me from the boys' line.

I waved back at him.

"Hey, you!" he said.

"What?"

He pointed to the boys' line. "Come over here!"

I went over.

"That's better," he said.

"What's better?" I asked.

"You have to stand in the boys' line," he told me.

"I do?" I looked at the girls' line. All the girls were standing over there.

"Of course," said the boy in the baseball cap like mine. "You're a boy."

"I'm not a boy," I said.

The boy looked at me. "Yes, you are."

"No, I'm not."

He pointed at my shoes. "You have on boys' sneakers." He pointed at my cap. "You have a boy's cap."

"These are my sneakers and my cap," I said. "I'm a girl! Okay?"

He pointed at my ears. "You have a boy's haircut."

"This is not a boy's haircut!" I said. "This is *my* haircut."

The principal pointed at us. "Please get in line," he said.

I went to the girls' line.

The boy called out after me, "You're stupid!"

"Why did he call you stupid?" said the girl in front of me.

"He wants me to get in the boys' line," I said.

"Maybe you should," said the girl.

Oh, brother! I thought.

The bell rang. We all walked inside. The boy with the cap like mine pushed my arm.

"Stop pushing," I said.

"You're stupid," he said.

"I am not."

"Are too," said the boy in the cap just like mine. "You're a boy. But you say you're a girl. That's stupid."

3
The Letter

Every day I stood in the girls' line. Every day the boy called me stupid. He wasn't in my class. But I found out his name was Jerry. Jerry and the other boys talked about me.

"She has a boy's backpack."

"She has boys' hair."

"She wears boys' jeans."

"She has to be a boy."

I heard them. But I didn't say anything. Mommy had said to ignore them.

But I was getting mad.

Then a boy from my class called me "George." His name was Michael.

I was walking down the hall.

"Hi, George," Michael said.

"My name is Georgia," I told him. He knew that. Everyone in my class knew that by now.

"Your real name is George," said Michael. "You're a boy. A boy who's so stupid that he says that he's really a girl."

My feelings were getting hurt. I was almost crying. "You're dumb!" I told Michael. "And your name is Michelle!"

"My name is not Michelle!" Michael shouted.

"Yes it is!" I yelled.

Just then Mr. Jones, our teacher, came out to the hall.

"What's the problem?" he asked.

"She called me Michelle," said Michael.

"That's because you called me George," I said. Now I was crying. I couldn't help it.

Mr. Jones looked at Michael. "Were you teasing her?"

"She's not a 'her,'" said Michael. "She's a *'him.'*"

"Go into the classroom," Mr. Jones said to Michael.

Then I told Mr. Jones about Jerry. Jerry was the one who had started it. Jerry had called me stupid. Jerry had told Michael and the other boys that I wasn't a girl.

"I ought to know whether I'm a boy or a girl," I told Mr. Jones.

"Write a letter to Jerry's teacher," said Mr. Jones. "I'll help you."

So we did. Jerry's teacher was named Mrs. Weintraub.

Dear Mrs. Weintraub,
 Your student named Jerry is always bothering me. I am a girl and I told him so. But he keeps saying that I am a boy pretending to be a girl. A girl can wear jeans and have a short haircut and do anything else she wants to, as long as she's not breaking the law. Please tell Jerry to stop.

Yours truly,
Georgia

I gave the letter to Mrs. Weintraub, and she showed the letter to Jerry. Mr. Jones and Mrs. Weintraub and Jerry and I met out in the hall. Jerry said that he wouldn't bother me anymore…even though he still thought that I looked like a boy.

4
Rose

My new school had a climber. I climbed to the top and jumped down.

I hung upside down on the monkey bars.

One day at the swings, I met a girl named Rose.

"Are you a boy or a girl?" she asked.

Rose had on jeans like me. But she was wearing earrings.

"I'm a girl," I said.

Rose said, "Oh." Then she said, "Why do you play boys' games?"

"I don't play boys' games," I said.

"You jump down from the climber," said Rose. "That's what the boys like to do."

"I like to do it, too," I said. "So maybe it's a girls' game."

"Maybe," said Rose. "But I think you should grow your hair."

I went home. I looked at my ears. I told Mommy what Rose had said.

"I know what," said Mommy. "How about some earrings? Maybe then people will stop asking you if you're a girl or a boy."

I tried Mommy's earrings on. "Could I wear just one earring?" I said. "Then I would look like a pirate."

"Maybe we should forget the earrings," Mommy said. "But you could wear a dress."

"No way!" I said.

"Why not?" said Mommy.

"Because," I said, "people will look under it."

"No, they won't," said Mommy.

"They will!" I said. "They will look when I jump off the climber."

"When your hair grows out," said Mommy, "things will be better."

"I don't think so," I said.

"Why not?" asked Mommy.

"Because when my hair grows out, my neck will be hot."

5
Robin

In the cafeteria I met Robin. Robin had long hair. Robin had a blue lunchbox, just like mine.

I had never seen Robin before. Not even in line.

"I like your lunchbox," I said.

"I like *your* lunchbox," said Robin. "Is your lunchbox good for drumming on? Mine is."

Robin began to drum.

"Hey, that's nice," I said, drumming on mine. "I think my lunchbox is good for drumming on, too."

I asked, "Do you play baseball?"

Robin said, "Sometimes. But I like to draw, too."

Robin and I finished eating lunch.
Then we went outside to the playground.
We climbed up on the climber and then
jumped off.

On the monkey bars, Robin and I

hung upside down. We really liked that.

"What else do you like to do?" I asked.
"Do you like to sing in the shower?"

"Yes! I love to sing in the shower,"
said Robin.

We sat down on the swings.

"Are you a boy or a girl?" asked Robin.

"A girl."

"You can't be," said Robin.

"Why not?"

"Because I'm a boy. And you're my new friend."

"You're a boy?" I said.

"Of course I am," said Robin.

"You have long hair," I said.

"And your hair is short," Robin pointed out.

I laughed. "I thought you were a girl."

Robin laughed. "I thought *you* were a boy."

"Just goes to show," I said.

"Goes to show what?" asked Robin.

"A girl can have short hair. A boy can have long hair. And a girl and a boy can be friends."

6
The Big Question

After school, Robin and I walked home.
But first we stopped at the candy store.

At the candy store there was one big
line. All the people who wanted to buy
something stood in the same line.

Some kids came up to Robin and me.

"Are you a girl?" one of the kids asked
Robin.

"No," said Robin, "I'm a boy."

The kid touched Robin on the head.
"What's this, then?"

"That's my hair," said Robin. "Don't
touch!"

The kid kept on touching.

So Robin pushed him!

Then somebody else snatched my cap
off my head!

"Hey!" I said.

"Are you a boy or a girl?" this kid said.

"She's a girl!" a loud voice yelled.

It was Rose! Only now Rose had short
hair!

Rose took my cap away from the kid
and gave it back to me.

"Mind your own beeswax!" Rose said.

Robin and Rose and I left the store.

"People are dumb," said Robin.

"Don't they have anything better to do?" said Rose.

"Your hair looks good that way," I told her.

"Thanks," Rose said. "It's like yours."

Now I play with Robin and Rose.

We jump off the climber. We swing and we draw.

Sometimes we sing a song together.

Once we even played baseball with Michael. And he didn't call me George.

Sometimes, people still ask me the big question.

"Are you a boy or a girl?"

Most of them already know, but they ask anyway. Just because.

A lot of people are getting to know me. Soon everybody in the school will know who I am!

I think that's pretty good for somebody who just moved here.

My hair is growing.

So tomorrow I'm getting a haircut.

"Are you sure you want to do that?"
asked Mommy.

I'm sure. I like short hair. Especially
on me. And on Rose. But not on Robin.
Because Robin likes his hair long. So I
hope he never gets a haircut.

There's a girl in my class named
Susan.

"Are you a tomboy?" she asked.

"I'm *no* kind of boy," I answered.
"I'm just my own kind of girl."